To..
....
....

This book invites you
to a Halloween Scare

Prepare If You Dare

A Halloween
Scare in
MINNESOTA

To my own little monster, Max, and his marvellous mum x

Visit the author's website! http://ericjames.co.uk

Written by Eric James
Illustrated by Marina Le Ray, Stefano Azzalin
and Natalie & Tamsin Hinrichsen
Designed by Sarah Allen

Published by Sourcebooks Jabberwocky, an imprint of Sourcebooks, Inc.
P.O. Box 4410, Naperville, Illinois 60567-4410
(630) 961-3900
Fax: (630) 961-2168
www.jabberwockykids.com

Library of Congress Cataloging-in-Publication data is on file with the publisher.

Date of Production: April 2016
Run Number: HTW_PO080316
Printed and bound in China (LPG)
10 9 8 7 6 5 4 3

Prepare If You Dare

A Halloween
Scare in
MINNESOTA

Written by Eric James
Illustrated by Marina Le Ray

Ş sourcebooks
jabberwocky

Prepare, if you dare,
for a night full of thrills,
The time **Minnesota** gave everyone chills,

A tale filled with sights that are best left unseen.
You ready? You sure?
This was my Halloween.

The werewolves
howled loudly.
The moon shone so bright.
I stayed in my bedroom,
the curtains shut tight.

My heart started pounding,
my knees felt so weak,
But, being a brave kid,
I just **had** to peek.

I pulled back the curtains. My mouth opened wide.
An army of monsters had gathered outside!
They staggered and stumbled and lurched down the streets
With bags full of cookies and candy corn treats.

Emerging from sewers and houses and stores
Came creatures and critters with ravenous roars.
Then more came along from all over the state.
They filled up the streets at a dizzying rate!

From **Bloomington**, **Plymouth**, **Duluth**, and **Saint Paul**,
The big and the little, the tall and the small,

All gathered together
for one **spooky** night,
To seek out the living
and give them a **fright.**

The thunder clapped loudly with terrible booms.
The witches dodged lightning and clung to their brooms.
The two-headed doggies tried chasing their tails,
And banshees let loose with their hideous wails.

The vampires hung out
on the street in their gangs,
And grinned, just to show off
their pearly white fangs.

JUST
MARRIED IN
MINNESOTA

The mummies moaned loudly and swayed side to side,
While Frankenstein stomped about town with his bride.

The Vikings rose up from the frostbitten ground
To pillage and plunder and rampage through town.
While smelling of lutefisk and dizzy with drink,
They tried to cause trouble but just caused a stink.

The starving young ogres who wandered the plains
Came looking for food, as they had hunger pains.
They climbed up the red pines, and hid out of view,
Then jumped down to scare passers-by with a "BOO!"

The creepies were crawly, the crazies were crazed,
The Rochester zombies had eyes that were glazed.
The ogres from Moorhead were ugly as sin,
With big bulging noses and warts on their chin.

The ghouls danced around but were lacking in soul,
The gargoyles could rock, and the headless could roll!
Although the whole spectacle seemed to spell doom,
I foolishly thought I'd be safe in my room!

But then something happened
that made my heart jump.
From somewhere below me
I heard a big THUMP!

I froze for a moment, as quiet as a mouse.
Yes, I could hear noises from INSIDE THE HOUSE!

I put on my slippers

and pulled on my robe.

I shook like a leaf

but I don't think it showed.

Then, slowly but surely,

I crept down the stairs,

Preparing myself for the
biggest of scares.

SPLIT ROCK LIGHTHOUSE

My hands trembled wildly.
I opened the door.
I still shudder now
at the horrors I saw.
The stereo spat out
some hideous sounds
As dozens of monsters
jumped madly around.

The sight was horrific. It made my skin crawl.
These monsters were having their

Halloween Ball!

I ♥ MINNESOTA

And right in the middle, one monster loomed tall,
The hairiest, scariest monster of all...

He turned round and saw me.
I fell to my knees.
"I'm not very tasty,
so don't eat me, please!"

He beamed ear-to-ear
and broke free from the huddle,

Ran over,
and gave me a...

BIG

MONSTER

CUDDLE!

"At last!

We have found you!" he said with a smile.
"From Marshall to Hibbing,
we've looked for a while.

BEST
COSTUME
IN

MINNESOTA

I ♥ MINNESO

"We came here to give you your wonderful prize."
He held up a trophy in front of my eyes.

"A prize? And for me?"

I replied with a grin.
"But what did I enter and how did I win?"
"You've won the first prize for the costume you're wearing!
It even scares me, and I'm tip-top at scaring!"

"This isn't a costume. I'm just dressed as me!"

"Exactly, the scariest thing you can be!

A small human child, with a cute button nose.

Your teeth are so shiny, you've only ten toes.

No hair on your face and no horns on your head.

The whites of your eyes are not glowing or red!

A bone-chilling costume! A horrible sight!

A worthy ensemble
for Halloween night!"

We partied together
until the moon set,
A Halloween night
that I'll never forget.

And next year I won't
want to hide in my bed.
The monsters won't scare me,